Pretty Please

A Book of Manners

New York

Printed in China

First Edition

1   3   5   7   9   10   8   6   4   2

Library of Congress Catalog Card Number: 2004112391

ISBN: 0-7868-3614-8

For more Disney Press fun, visit www.disneybooks.com

WALT DISNEY'S
Snow White
and the Seven Dwarfs

How to Eat
Like a Princess

BREE

Snow White had just arrived at the Seven Dwarfs' cottage. She cooked a big pot of delicious-smelling soup for dinner, and everyone was hungry. But just as they were about to sit down and eat, Snow White noticed something.

"Your hands!" she cried.

The Dwarfs looked down at their hands. "What's wrong with 'em?" Grumpy snapped.

"They're so *dirty*!" Snow White exclaimed. "Please go and wash at once. We cannot eat until you do."

The Dwarfs grumbled, but they did as she said. After all, she *was* a princess.

"Be sure to use warm water," Snow White reminded them. "And lots of soap!"

When the Dwarfs were clean, they hurried back inside. "I'll set the table!" Happy declared. He got to work.

"Oh, dear," said Snow White, when the table was set. "Something's not quite right here!"

So, Snow White taught the Dwarfs
how to set the table properly.

The fork
goes on
the left.

The plate
goes in the
middle.

The knife
and spoon go
on the right.

The napkin
can be tucked
under the fork.

"Don't forget your napkin," Snow White said, once everyone was seated. "It goes in your lap."

Finally, it was time to eat. The Dwarfs were very excited to be dining with a princess. In fact, Happy was so distracted that he forgot his manners and reached across the table to get some food.

"Happy," scolded Doc, "you ought to say, 'Fleas pass the please.' Er, I mean, 'Cheese pass the knees.' I mean—"

"He means," said Sneezy, "'Please pass the peas.'
Ah-ah-ah-CHOO!"

"Cover your mouth when you sneeze!"
cried Grumpy.

The Seven Dwarfs learned a few
more important things that night, like
keep your mouth closed when you're
chewing your food . . .

. . . say "excuse me" if you burp . . .

. . . and it's just plain dopey to play with your food.

Snow White just giggled. She knew what was different: royally good manners make everything taste better!

It's Nice to Be Nice

It was the day of Cinderella and Prince Charming's wedding. Everyone in the kingdom had turned up for the joyous celebration. Cinderella's stepsisters, Anastasia and Drizella, were there, too. But they were feeling more jealous than joyous.

"It's not fair that Cinderella is marrying the Prince," Anastasia whined.

"I don't understand why he likes her more than us," Drizella snapped. "After all, she isn't nearly as pretty as we are."

"That's true," Anastasia agreed.

"And she doesn't have my beautiful voice," said Drizella. "They say I sing as sweetly as a nightingale."

"I've been told my flute playing can make a grown man cry," Anastasia chimed in. "But Cinderella can't play any instrument at all. Why, she can't do anything but sweep and scrub. She's nothing more than a plain old housemaid!"

Cinderella's mouse friends overheard them.

"I know why the Prince likes Cinderelly," Jaq said.

"Me, too," said Gus. "And it doesn't have anything to do with playing a flute."

"That's right," said Jaq. "It's because Cinderelly would never say mean things about someone else."

"Plus, Cinderelly says 'please' when she wants something," Jaq pointed out.

"And 'thank you' when she gets it," Gus added.

"Some folks are awfully stingy with their pleases and thank-yous," Jaq noted.

"Cinderelly is always smiling," Gus continued. "She says hello to everyone she meets."

"That's true," said Jaq. "Not like *some* people who walk around with their noses in the air, thinking they are better than everyone else."

"And Cinderelly never calls people rotten names," Jaq continued.

Just then, the Grand Duke, who wasn't watching where he was going, accidentally bumped into Anastasia and Drizella.

"Watch it, you idiot!" Anastasia shrieked.

"Look out, you klutz!" Drizella snapped.

"I beg your pardon," the Grand Duke said.

Then the two sisters lifted their noses into the air and marched off in a huff.

Jaq and Gus just shook their heads. "I guess those two will never know why the Prince likes Cinderelly better," Jaq said.

"It's too bad they never asked us," said Gus. "We could have told them."

Boasting Is Boring

Gaston was at it again. "Did you know, Belle, that I won the barrel-lifting competition four years in a row?" he asked. "That's because I'm the strongest man in the whole village."

"Yes, Gaston," Belle replied. "You've already told me several times."

"And did you know that all the girls in the village think I am the handsomest fellow in town?" Gaston said. "They all want to go out with me."

Belle sighed and exchanged a look with her father. "Yes, Gaston," she said. "You already told me that, too."

"Also, I'm terrifically smart," Gaston went on. "When I was in school, I did better than anyone else on every test. Why, I don't think there's a soul around who can match my wits."

"You don't say," said Belle.

"And talk about fast," Gaston declared. "I can outrun any creature around—man, beast, or fowl."

Just then, a horse-drawn carriage went whizzing by.

"Why," Gaston continued, "I could even outrun that horse!"

"Really?" asked Belle.

"Absolutely!" cried Gaston. "Just watch!"

And to Belle's great relief, Gaston took off.

"Well," Belle's father said to her, "that was a stroke of luck! Gaston won't be back for some time. The closest village is twenty miles away!"

Belle smiled. "I know," she said. "That Gaston is such a bore.

It's nice to be proud of what you're good at, but what Gaston is *best* at is boasting. If he's as strong and handsome and clever and fast as he says he is," she added with a smile, "he should be perfectly happy keeping *himself* company for a while."

You should always be proud of yourself, but no one likes to be around someone who boasts. Here's a better way of saying what Gaston said. . . .

INSTEAD OF . . .   TRY . . .

Walt Disney's
Sleeping Beauty

The Ups and Downs
of Interrupting

One day, when Briar Rose came home from a walk in the woods, she felt very tired.

"Why don't you lie down and rest," her Aunt Flora suggested.

"I think that's a good idea," said Briar Rose, and she went to her room.

A few moments later, Fauna and Merryweather came bustling in the door. "Look!" Merryweather cried loudly. "We found mushrooms! Oh, what a delicious stew we'll have for dinner tonight!"

"Shhhh! Not so loud," Flora whispered. "Rose is resting. You must keep your voice down when someone is sick or sleeping."

"Oh, dear! Is she all right?" Merryweather
asked.

"Well, she's—" Flora began.

"What are her symptoms?" Fauna burst in.
"Does she have a fever? Could it be the flu?"

"Well, I—" Flora started to say.

"You don't suppose it's the mumps?" Fauna interrupted again. "Oh, the mumps are awful. Poor Rose!"

"Fauna," Flora snapped, "if you would stop interrupting, I could tell you that Briar Rose is fine, just a little tired. Now, both of you, stop talking and help me make the stew!"

Flora made the fire. But she didn't notice when a spark flew out and hit her skirt. Her dress began to smoke.

"Flora!" Merryweather yelled in alarm.

"Merryweather, what did I say about being quiet?" Flora scolded. "I told you that Briar Rose is sl—"

"But, Flora!" Fauna cried.

"Fauna, there you go again, interrupting," Flora said.

Luckily, at that moment, Briar Rose came into the kitchen.

"Oh, my goodness!" she cried. Quickly, she grabbed a bucket of water and doused Flora's skirt.

"Oh, my," Flora said. She turned to Fauna and Merryweather. "That's what you were trying to tell me, isn't it? I guess *sometimes* it's okay to be loud and to interrupt, after all."

Usually, it's not good to interrupt. But it's okay when there's an emergency. For example . . .

an angry bee . . .

an urgent message . . .

or a fire-breathing dragon.

Say You're Sorry

Ariel had disobeyed her father's orders and gone to the surface . . . again. When King Triton found out, he was furious.

"Ariel, from now on you may not go *anywhere* unless I say so!" he roared.

"You never let me do *anything*," she snapped back. "I wish . . . I wish you weren't my father!"

Ariel hadn't meant to say that, but she was angry
and it just slipped out.
King Triton looked at Ariel sadly and swam away.

Later, Sebastian and Flounder found Ariel crying. "What's wrong, child?" Sebastian asked.

Ariel sighed. "My father and I are always fighting," she said. "He yelled at me today and I yelled back. I think I hurt his feelings."

"Why don't you tell him you're sorry," Sebastian suggested.

"I . . . I don't know how," Ariel replied.

"Child, it's easy," said Sebastian. "You just look him in the eye and say, 'I'm sorry.'"

I'm sorry.

Beg your pardon.

"Are you sure?" asked Ariel. "That doesn't seem like enough."

"Oh, but it is," said Sebastian. "You don't want to make it too fancy. Keep it simple."

Too Fancy:

Magnificent King, I most humbly beg your forgiveness for my inconsiderate behavior . . .

Just Right:

I'm sorry.

"But what if he's still angry and doesn't listen?"
Ariel asked.

"Trust me, he will listen," Sebastian said. "And you'll
feel much better. Now, go and tell him."

"Just remember, Ariel," Sebastian called after her, "the most important thing . . ."

"... is that it comes from the heart."

Be a Good Guest

Princess Jasmine, Aladdin, and Abu had ridden the Magic Carpet to a faraway land, where everything seemed strange and new. When the king invited them to dinner, Aladdin was nervous.

"Everything here is different," he whispered to Jasmine. "What if I don't like the food? Or what if the king doesn't like *me*?"

"Don't worry, Aladdin," Jasmine said. "It's fun to go to new places and try new things. Just remember a few things when you're a guest in someone else's house."

"Try a little bit of everything on your plate," Jasmine suggested.

"If you already know you don't like something, you don't have to eat it. But don't say, 'yuck' or 'gross.' Just say, 'No, thank you,'" she advised.

"Be sure to say something nice to your hosts to let them know how much fun you had," Jasmine explained.

"And after you get home, don't forget to send a thank-you note," Jasmine said.

Jasmine's Tips for Thank-you Notes

 Start with a **greeting**. "Dear" comes first, followed by the name of the person you are writing to.

 The **body** of the letter is the part where you thank the person you are writing to. You can send a thank-you note when you've visited someone's house, when someone has sent you a gift, or anytime someone has done something nice for you.

 You can end the letter with a nice **closing**, such as "Sincerely," "Yours truly," "Your friend," or "Best wishes." If it's someone you know very well, you might even write "Love."

 Your **signature** goes at the end.

 Have an adult help you put it in an envelope and write the address. Don't forget the stamp!

FROM: *Princess Jasmine*

TO: *King Fluffinpuffer*

Dear King Fluffinpuffer,

Thank you for inviting me to your palace for dinner. I particularly enjoyed the roasted beets with marshmallow sauce—they were delicious! I hope that someday you can come visit my home in Agrabah.

Your friend,

Princess Jasmine

"So, you see," Jasmine told Aladdin, "there's nothing to worry about. If you follow a few simple rules, you know you'll always be invited back."

You're Invited!